GO, MO, GO!
SEASIDE SPRINT

HODDER CHILDREN'S BOOKS

First published in Great Britain in 2018 by Hodder and Stoughton

1 3 5 7 9 10 8 6 4 2

A CIP catalogue record for this book
is available from the British Library.

ISBN 978 1 444 93403 8

Printed and bound in Great Britain by
Clays Ltd, St Ives plc

The paper and board used in this book
are made from wood from responsible sources.

MIX
Paper from
responsible sources
FSC
www.fsc.org
FSC® C104740

Hodder Children's Books
An imprint of
Hachette Children's Group
Part of Hodder and Stoughton
Carmelite House
50 Victoria Embankment
London EC4Y 0DZ

An Hachette UK Company
www.hachette.co.uk

www.hachettechildrens.co.uk

GO, MO, GO!
SEASIDE SPRINT

Written by Kes Gray for

Mo Farah

Illustrations by Chris Jevons

Hodder
Children's
Books

It was a blisteringly beautiful, hot summer's day and Little Mo and his friends had taken a trip to the seaside.

"Are we going to go running today?" asked Lily, crouching down in the sand to retie the laces of her trainers.

"No," said Mo, blowing up a beach ball with ten big puffs and then tossing it for Lyra to catch.

Lyra caught the ball and clasped it to her chest.

"NO?" she frowned. "But we always go running!"

"YES WE ALWAYS GO RUNNING!" said Vern, receiving the ball from Lyra and then batting it on to Banjo. **"RUNNING IS WHAT WE DO!"**

"Not today," smiled Mo. "Today is a rest day. If we want to become better at running then it's important we become better at resting too. Rest days give the muscles in our legs time to recover from all the hard work we ask them to do."

"So the better we rest, the better we

run?" asked Vern, receiving the beach ball from Banjo and then batting it on to Lily.

"Absolutely," said Mo. **"Anyone fancy an ice cream?"**

Vern punched the air.

Lyra did a dance.

Banjo did a head over heels.

Lily caught the beach ball, tucked it under her arm and beamed.

EVERYONE fancied an ice cream!

"I love rest days!" said Lyra, scampering across the beach towards the ice cream van. "Especially rest days that include ice creams!"

Mo, Vern, Lily and Banjo smiled and followed Lyra across the sand.

"WALK, LYRA, REMEMBER!" laughed Mo. **"NO RUNNING FOR ANYONE TODAY!"**

"Sorry," said Lyra, slowing to a fast walk. "I forgot!"

By the time the five friends had reached the ice cream van they had already decided which ice cream they were going to ask for.

Well almost.

"A 99 please!" said Lily, placing her money on the counter.

"A 99 with an extra flake please," smiled Banjo.

"That's not fair," said Lily,

"I want an extra flake too!"

"I want an extra flake AND strawberry sauce on mine," said Vern.

"I want an extra flake, strawberry sauce AND chocolate sauce on mine," said Lyra.

"FIVE 99s, all with extra flakes, all with chocolate sauce **AND** strawberry sauce please," said Mo.

"And sprinkles if you've got them," said Banjo. **"Well, it IS a rest day!"**

Ice cream by ice cream, flake by flake, sauce by sauce and yes, sprinkle by sprinkle, five magnificent 99s appeared before them.

"ENJOY!" said the ice cream man, leaning from the window of his van and passing one to each of the five friends in turn.

"WE CERTAINLY WILL," they nodded, raising their 99s to eye level and deliberating over which bit to lick first.

"I'm going to nibble my chocolate flake …" said Lyra.

"I'm going to lick my chocolate sauce …" said Lily.

"I'm going for strawberry sauce …" murmured Vern

"Sprinkles for me!" smiled Banjo.

"RUN!" shouted Mo.

Lyra, Banjo, Vern and Lily wrenched their eyes from their ice creams and wheeled round in confusion. Instead of pointing his tongue in the direction of his 99, Mo was sprinting away from the ice cream van in the direction of the pier, arm

outstretched and his ice cream held aloft.

"Why are we running?" shouted Lyra, racing as fast as she could to catch him up.

"Yes, why are we running?" shouted Vern and Banjo. "We haven't had our first lick!"

"SEAGULLS!" shouted Mo, **"Seagulls have spotted our 99s!"**

Lily, Banjo, Lyra and Vern looked over

8

their shoulders. Mo was right, a flock
of hungry seagulls were dive-bombing
straight towards them.

"They must have spotted the extra
flakes!" shouted Lily.

"And the chocolate sauce," shouted
Vern.

"And the strawberry sauce," squealed
Lyra.

"And the sprinkles!" squeaked Banjo.

"Head for the pier!"

shouted Mo. "We can eat our 99s there!"

The pier was the perfect place to hide. It stretched a mile out to sea and had a strict **no seagull admission policy**. All the five friends had to do was reach it in time!

Heads down, arms outstretched, ice creams held aloft, they raced across the sand.

"I hope my flakes don't fall out!" shouted Vern, trying his best to balance his ice cream and run at the same time.

"ME TOO!" said Banjo, waving a marauding seagull away with his free hand.

Across the beach they raced, up some steps, past the candy floss stall and through the entrance to the pier.

The instant the five friends vanished from view, the chief seagull gave the signal to about-turn.

"SCREECH!" it squawked, applying the brakes in midair and soaring away from the pier entrance.

"We've lost them!" cheered Lyra, sprinting past the fudge stall.

"We've outrun them!" whooped Banjo, bounding past the bouncy castle.

"Keep running to the end of the pier," shouted Mo. **"We can shelter in the amusement arcade**

and polish off our ice creams there!"

Past the merry-go-round, past the tea cups, through the bowling alley they sprinted …

"It's easier running across piers than it is on sand!" whooped Lyra, finding a completely new spring in her step.

"Sand really slows you down!" shouted Vern, equally pleased to be on firm ground.

"There's the arcade!" cheered Lily, bounding past

Candy Floss & Popcorn

the ghost train and pointing the way
with her 99.

"At last!" cheered Vern.
"Ice creams here
we come!"

With their feathery foes defeated and their 99s still intact, the five friends gathered by the penny falls.

"Mmmm," drooled Banjo, turning his attention to his sprinkles.

"Yum," smiled Lyra, raising her cone to eye level and getting ready to demolish some chocolate sauce.

"RUN!" shouted **Mo,** wheeling around suddenly and sprinting away from the arcade.

Lyra, Banjo, Lily and Vern lowered their 99s and stared in disbelief.

"But you said it was a **REST DAY!**" they gasped. "Why do you want us to run?"

"The ghosts in the ghost train have spotted us!" shouted Mo. "And they fancy an ice cream too!"

Mo was right. Four ghostly pirates and a phantom mermaid were floating straight towards them, arms outstretched and tongues dangling.

"I've never seen a ghost before!" shivered Banjo, raising his 99 aloft and chasing after Mo.

"Ghosts have never seen 99s like THESE before!" shouted Mo, dodging a swipe from a ghostly cutlass.

Mo was right. The ghosts who had spotted them from the ghost train had five things on their mind and five things only:

ICE CREAM,
CHOCOLATE FLAKES,
STAWBERRY SAUCE,
CHOCOLATE SAUCE
AND SPRINKLES.

"I'm not sharing my ice cream with a phantom mermaid!" said Lily, dodging a swipe from a ghostly mermaid tail.

"Or a spooky pirate," shouted Vern, leaping the outstretched hurdle of a ghostly wooden leg.

"Maybe if we told them where the ice cream van is, they could **buy their own**," gasped Banjo, evading the clutches of some **ghostly pirate fingers**.

"Too risky!" shouted Mo. **"Just keep RUNNING!"**

Past the ghost train, through the bowling alley, and round the teacups, they sprinted.

"They're still behind us!" gulped Lyra, glancing over her shoulder.

"LOOK AT THE SIZE OF THEIR TONGUES!!!!!"

Lyra was right, the 99s they had bought from the ice cream van were **such magnificent sights to behold**, no ghost was going to give them up lightly.

"We need to get into the daylight fast!" hollered Mo. "Ghosts might like

99s but they don't like daylight at all. Especially bright sunlight!"

Heads down, arms outstretched, ice creams melting, the five friends hurtled on, past the merry-go-round, past the bouncy castle, round the fudge stall and out through the exit of the pier.

21

"Keep running!" said Mo, darting sharply right by the Punch and Judy show and sprinting further along the promenade.

Vern, Lily, Banjo and Lyra raised their ice creams longingly and followed hot on Mo's tail.

"Are the ghosts still chasing us?" panted Vern, hardly daring to look round.

"I don't think so," panted Lyra, risking a quick glance over her shoulder and then slowing down with relief.

To everyone's relief the spooks had returned empty handed to the ghost train. The daylight had done the job just as Mo had promised it would.

"No sign of any seagulls either!" panted Vern, shielding the sunlight from his eyes and scanning the sky for greedy beaks.

With the coast clear and a view out to sea beckoning, the five friends made their way further down the promenade to a wooden bench facing invitingly out to sea. Bottoms parked, ice creams raised, they got ready to enjoy their first lick.

"RUN!"
shouted Mo,

springing up from the bench and pointing back towards the pier.

"BUT WE'VE ONLY JUST SAT DOWN!" winced Lily. **"WHY DO WE NEED TO RUN NOW?!"**

"The dodgem cars have broken loose from the dodgem track," said Mo. **"And they're heading straight for us!"**

Lily, Banjo, Vern and Lyra lowered their ice creams in despair and stared goggle-eyed down the road.

Sparks flying, bumpers bumping, a grand prix of driverless dodgem cars was veering and swerving wildly out of control along the entire length of the seafront road!

"But I thought dodgem cars needed electricity to make them go?" squeaked Lyra, leaping to her feet.

"AND DRIVERS!" exclaimed Vern, turning tail with his 99. "How can they go anywhere without drivers?"

"SOLAR POWERED!" shouted Mo." THESE

DODGEMS ARE SOLAR POWERED!!!"

Heads down, arms outstretched, ice creams dripping, the five friends ran full pelt along the seafront to escape the dodgems.

"How fast can dodgem cars go?" gasped Lyra, glancing over her shoulder at a fast-approaching bumper.

"On a day as hot as this, SUPER FAST!" shouted Mo.

"What side of the road are they driving?!" gasped Lily, snaking left and right along the seafront in an attempt to avoid being hit.

"BOTH SIDES!" shouted Mo. "MAKE SURE YOU LOOK BACK IN BOTH DIRECTIONS AS YOU RUN!"

Heads down, arms outstretched, ice creams dripping, flakes drooping, the five friends continued their race along the seafront. With every passing second, the red, green, yellow and blue bonnets of the dodgem cars drew menacingly and dangerously closer. With every puff and pant their lungs could muster, the five friends hurtled on.

Down the seafront, through the traffic lights, and over the roundabout they raced.

"Where are the traffic police when you need them?!" panted Banjo. "The speed limit along this promenade is only **20MPH!** They must be doing sixty at least!"

"Cross your fingers they'll all get punctures!" gasped Lily, putting on a spurt as a bumper drew too close for comfort.

"Dodgem cars don't get punctures!" squeaked Lyra, zigzagging in every direction she could think of to try and shake off the car chasing her. "No wheels means no punctures!" she gasped.

"IF WE CAN'T OUTRUN THEM, WE NEED TO

OUTSMART THEM," shouted Mo. **"Head for the lighthouse, we'll be safe from dodgem cars there!"**

Lily, Vern, Banjo and Lyra raised their ice creams even higher and found another gear. Heads down, arms outstretched, ice creams dripping, flakes drooping, cones crumpling, the five friends followed hot on Mo's heels, past the lifeboat station, along the coastal path, through the tufty dunes and all the way to the lighthouse door.

"If the stairs of the lighthouse don't stop those crazy dodgems, the edge of the cliff top will!" Mo shouted.

Mo was right. One by one, the out-of-control dodgems either crashed at the foot of the lighthouse stairs or hurtled over the cliff top to the watery car park below.

"That was close," gasped Lily.

"TOO CLOSE," wheezed Banjo.

"Boy am I ready for an ice cream now!" gasped Vern.

"How many steps are there to the top?" asked Lyra. "I'm looking forward to a 99 with a view!"

"Let's count them as we go!" beckoned Mo with a bound.

There were a lot of stairs to count.

"657," panted Lily.

"I made it 656," panted Vern.

"I lost count at 346," gasped Lyra.

"Lily was right!" smiled Mo. "There are 657 steps to the top of this lighthouse!"

"I need to rest," said Mo, leaning against the guard rail that circled the lighthouse wall.

"We can see for miles!" smiled Lyra, gazing out to sea. "What a wonderful place to enjoy a 99!"

"I'm not sure my 99 looks like a 99 any more," frowned Banjo. **"It's gone all soggy."**

"My strawberry sauce looks more like chocolate sauce now," frowned Lyra.

"My sprinkles have completely dissolved," sighed Lily.

"I'm sure they will taste the same if we just close our eyes and lick," smiled Lyra.

"Good idea," nodded Lily, closing her eyes and poking out the tip of her tongue.

"Excellent idea," nodded Vern and Banjo, shutting their eyes fast too and raising their 99s to their lips.

"Ice creams, here we come!" swooned Vern.

"RUN!" shouted Mo.

Vern, Lyra, Banjo and Lily opened their eyes, zipped up their lips and sprang to attention again.

"WHAT NOW?!" they gasped.

"TIDAL
WAVE!"
pointed Mo.

"Look, a giant tidal wave is heading straight for the beach!"

Lyra, Vern, Banjo and Lily stared far out to sea. Sure enough, far out on the distant horizon a monstrous tidal wave was looming.

"How big do tidal waves get?" gasped Vern, lowering his 99 to chest height.

"Big enough to drown a house," gulped Lyra.

"Big enough to swallow a pier," winced Lily.

"Big enough to soak a seagull," said Banjo, "even when it's in midair!"

"If it's heading for the beach, then it's heading

for the town!" frowned Mo. **"We need to warn everyone that a tidal wave is coming!"**

"AND WE NEED TO DO IT FAST!"

"But what about our ice creams?" moped Banjo. "I was about to have my first lick!"

"RUN FIRST, LICK LATER!" said Mo, sprinting to the top of the lighthouse stairs.

Lyra, Lily, Banjo and Vern looked despairingly at their 99s and then followed Mo sadly.

"If we head for the bingo hall we can use the bingo caller's microphone to make an emergency announcement!" said Mo.

Heads down, arms outstretched, ice creams dribbling, flakes wilting,

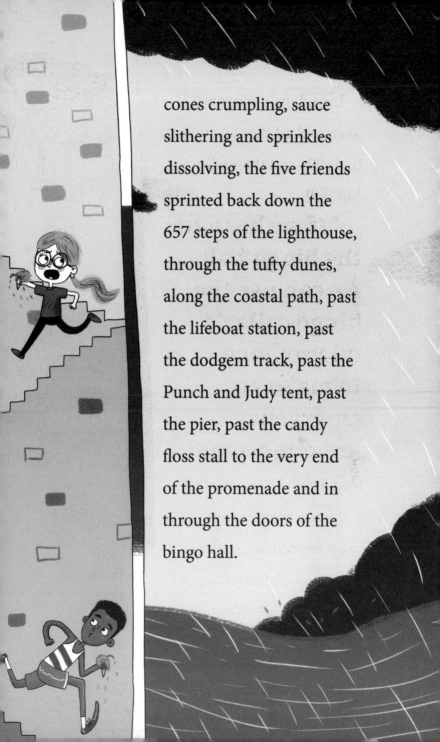

cones crumpling, sauce slithering and sprinkles dissolving, the five friends sprinted back down the 657 steps of the lighthouse, through the tufty dunes, along the coastal path, past the lifeboat station, past the dodgem track, past the Punch and Judy tent, past the pier, past the candy floss stall to the very end of the promenade and in through the doors of the bingo hall.

"TIDAL WAVE!" shouted Mo,

grabbing the bingo caller's microphone

and turning the volume up to FULL.

Bingo cards scattered like confetti as bingo players **dived under their tables for cover**.

The bingo caller boarded up his bingo hall in a flash. News of the approaching tidal wave spread even faster.

"I can hear it coming!" gulped Lily, crouching beneath a table with her ice cream in one hand.

Lily was right, a sky-scraping wall of water was rumbling closer with every second.

"It's getting nearer," squeaked Lily, as the floor began to shake.

"It's getting louder," squeaked Lyra, as her 99 began to shake too.

"BRACE YOURSELF!" said Mo, assuming the tidal-wave-approaching crouched position.

"I can't swim!" squeaked Banjo.

"I need my goggles!" whimpered Vern.

"BOOOOOM" thundered the tidal wave, crashing on

to the shore with the weight of a zillion elephants.

"MOOOOOB" it thundered in reverse, as the ebb flow returned the mighty wave far back out to sea.

"Has it gone?" whispered Lily, opening her eyes to find that her ice cream had finally stopped shaking.

"It's gone!" smiled Mo, crawling out from under the table with his 99 still held aloft. **"And we've saved the town!"** he grinned.

"We didn't even get wet!" cheered Banjo, wriggling out on both elbows.

"You did get chocolate flake all over your T-shirt though!" laughed Vern.

"And you did get strawberry sauce all over your cheek!" laughed Lyra.

"It's hard hiding under a table while you're holding a super squishy ice cream," laughed Mo.

"Especially super squishy squashy yucky mucky ice creams that are shaking as you hold them!" chuckled Lyra.

"Now let's go outside and enjoy them!"

Mo, Lyra, Vern, Lily and Banjo shook hands with the bingo caller and stepped back out on to the promenade. Thanks to the super-hot sunshine the seafront was drying out fast!

"I think we deserve an ice cream after that!" Banjo laughed, raising his 99 to his lips.

"What causes tidal waves?" asked Lily, targeting her 99 with her tongue.

"RUN!" shouted Mo.

Vern, Lyra, Banjo and Lily stared open-jawed as Mo suddenly set off running **AGAIN!**

"I'LL TELL YOU WHAT CAN CAUSE A TIDAL WAVE!" Mo shouted back over shoulder. **"A SEA MONSTER CAN CAUSE A TIDAL WAVE!!"**

Lily, Banjo, Lyra and Vern looked towards the beach. To their horror, a giant sea monster had emerged from the sea, dripping with seaweed and encrusted with limpets.

"It's taller than a lighthouse!" gasped Vern.

"It's longer than a train!" gasped Banjo.

"What if sea monsters like eating children as much as children like eating 99s?" gulped Lyra.

"RUN!"
shouted Lily.

"RUN!"
shouted Banjo.

"RUN!"

shouted Vern.

Heads down, arms held aloft, ice creams disintegrating, flakes squidging, cones gunging, sauce sloshing and sprinkles splurging, the five friends turned tail and sprinted away from the sea monster.

"It's following us!" gasped Lyra, glancing wide-eyed over her shoulder.

"It's catching up with us!" gasped Lily, feeling the ground shake with every giant stride the monster took.

The chase was on, but for every twenty strides Mo and his friends were taking, the sea monster was taking **ONE!**

"What if it catches us?" gasped Vern.

"What if it EATS US?" squealed Lily.

"Thank goodness it isn't wearing trainers," shouted Banjo. "If it was wearing trainers, we wouldn't stand a chance!"

"Follow me to Smugglers' Cove!" shouted Mo. **"We can hide**

from the sea monster in the secret cave and eat our ice creams there!"

Lily, Lyra, Banjo and Vern puffed out their cheeks and kicked again, back along the promenade, past the bingo hall, past the pier, past the lighthouse, down to the cove, over twelve sea walls, six rock pools and a very surprised crab and into Smugglers' Cove.

"It's still chasing us!" squeaked Vern, feeling the monstrous footsteps of the sea monster punch into the wet sand behind them.

"I can hear it slobbering!" gasped Lyra.

"I can hear it snuffling!" gasped Lily.

"And snorting!" panted Vern.

"And dribbling!" wheezed
Banjo.

"KEEP RUNNING!"
shouted Mo. **"WE'VE NEARLY
REACHED THE SECRET
CAVE!"**

Lily, Banjo, Lyra and Vern ran like they
had never run before.

"It's taller than the cliff top!" gasped
Banjo, glancing over his shoulder.

"It could swallow us whole!" gasped Lyra.

"And sideways," whimpered Banjo.

"NEARLY THERE!" shouted
Mo. **"NEARLY SAFE!"**

The five exhausted friends kicked again.
Across sand, across pebbles, through

puddles, around rocks, over rock pools, through surf and along the base of the towering cliff face in the direction of the secret cave.

"ALMOST THERE!" panted Mo.

"ALMOST SAFE!" wheezed Banjo. "Not breakfast," he gasped.

"OH NO!" cried Mo, slamming his heels into the sand. **"THE ENTRANCE TO THE SECRET CAVE IS BLOCKED BY FALLEN BOULDERS!"**

It was the worst news the five friends trying to escape a sea monster could receive. Not only was the secret cave blocked but they had run out of places to run.

"The tidal wave must have dislodged them!" groaned Banjo. **"We're sea monster breakfast for sure!"**

Lungs bursting, pulses racing, cheeks burning, hearts thumping, ice creams dissolving, held aloft, Vern, Lily, Lyra and Banjo dropped to their knees. **The wall of boulders before them was too high to climb, too heavy to move and too everything else to do anything about at all.**

Slowly, bravely the five friends turned to face the sea monster.

Its eyes were as deep as rock pools.

Its nostrils were as hollow as sea caves.

Its breath had the **unmistakeable reek of winkles and shrimps.**

"Hello," said the sea monster. "Has anyone lost a beach ball?"

Lyra turned to Banjo.

Banjo turned to Lily.

Lily turned to Vern.

Everyone turned to Mo.

"Er ... did you say beach ball?" asked Mo, not sure what else to say.

"Yes this one here," said the sea monster, producing a beach ball from behind his back and spinning it like a basketball on one claw.

"Only I saw you playing with one just like this on the beach earlier and I wondered if it might be yours?"

Mo turned to Vern.

Vern turned to Lily.

Lily turned to Banjo.

Banjo turned to Lyra.

Lily looked under her arm.

Sure enough, the beach ball she had tucked under there earlier that morning most certainly wasn't there now.

"I must have dropped it when we ran from the ice cream van," she squeaked.

"So it is yours!" beamed the

sea monster. "Oh that's such good news, only it's such a lovely beach ball, such lovely colours, don't you agree, when I found it floating far, far, far, far out to sea, I just had to try and return it. Sorry about the tidal wave by the way, I hope I didn't cause too much mess?"

"Aren't you going to eat us?" asked Banjo.

"Don't give him ideas!" whispered Mo, with a nudge.

"EAT YOU? Goodness no," said the sea monster, "it's winkles and shrimps for me. And razor clams on my birthday."

It wasn't quite the kind of sea monster

that any of the five friends had imagined. In fact it was a very nice sea monster indeed!

"It's very kind of you to return it to us," said Mo, stepping forward to reclaim the ball.

"Yes, and thanks for not eating us too," smiled Banjo.

"The pleasure is all mine," said the sea monster. "Perhaps next time you come to the seaside, you might consider tying your beach ball to a piece of string. One gust of wind, you know, and it could be gone again just like that! You can never be too careful with a beach ball, you know. Especially at the seaside on a beautiful day like this."

"We promise to be careful," nodded Mo.

"Well Lily does," frowned Banjo with an accusatory glance.

"Oh and one other thing," said the sea monster, "before I swim off back to sea."

"What's that?" asked Mo.

"How much are the ice creams?" asked the sea monster. "I would so like to try one."

Mo looked at Lyra.

Lyra looked at Banjo.

Banjo looked at Lily.

Lily looked at Vern.

Everyone looked at their ice creams.

"You can have ours if you like," said Mo.

"What's left of them," smiled Banjo.

"Really!" smiled the sea monster. "They do look delicious, all squidgy and squodgy and slishy and slushy. What do those lovely colours taste of?"

"That's meant to be chocolate sauce," said Lily, pointing to most areas of her 99.

"And this is meant to be strawberry sauce," said Lyra.

"These started off as chocolate flakes," said Banjo, wiping his T-shirt.

"And once upon a time these used to be sprinkles," chuckled Vern.

"How delicious," drooled the sea monster, opening his mouth, unfurling

his tongue and flopping it on to the sand.

"Here you go," smiled Mo, wiping the remains of his 99 on to the soft pink licky bit in the middle.

"Enjoy!" giggled Banjo, Lily, Lyra and Vern, adding their ice creams and then jumping back as the sea monster despatched them with a whip crack of his tongue.

"**Heavenly!**" the sea monster smiled, raising his head to cliff top height and then peering out to sea. "Well, I really must be going."

The five friends gathered on the shoreline and began waving their goodbyes to their new sea buddy.

"THANKS FOR RETURNING OUR BEACH BALL!" called Mo as the sea monster returned to the sea and disappeared beneath the waves. **"WE HOPE YOU ENJOYED YOUR REWARD!"**

"I never knew sea monsters liked ice creams," said Vern, turning back to the shore.

"I never knew they played basketball either!" frowned Banjo, trying without success to spin the beach ball on his finger.

"I guess sea monsters can be full of surprises," said Lily.

"Especially ice cream-loving sea monsters," smiled Vern.

"Now then," said Mo, beginning the long walk back to the seafront. **"What does everyone want to do now?"**

Lyra looked at Vern.

Vern looked at Banjo.

Banjo looked at Lily.

"Can we go home please, Mo?" said Vern.

"Yes can we go home?" everyone agreed. "We've had quite enough rest for one day!"

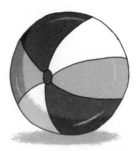

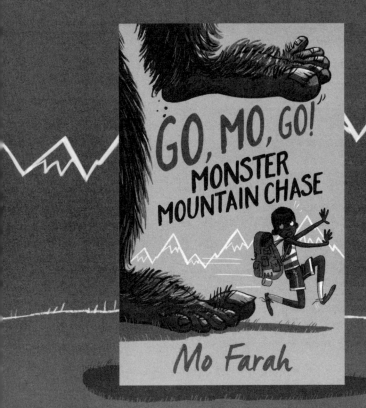

"I bet the Rocky Mountains rock!"

Mo and his friends are excited for a mountain adventure, until they find out that the Rocky Mountains really do rock – from *side* to *side* ...

But what is making the ground shake?

Watch out, here comes a HUGE HAIRY FOOT ...

RUN!

"Let's run like we've never run before!"

Mo and his friends are excited to discover a new way to run - backwards in time!

But what is that loud roaring noise behind them? Watch out, here comes a MASSIVE SCALY FOOT ...

RUN!